The Emperor
Strikes Out

Helaine Becker

Illustrated by
Sampar

Scholastic Canada Ltd.
Toronto New York London Auckland Sydney
Mexico City New Delhi Hong Kong Buenos Aires

Scholastic Canada Ltd.
604 King Street West, Toronto, Ontario M5V 1E1, Canada

Scholastic Inc.
557 Broadway, New York, NY 10012, USA

Scholastic Australia Pty Limited
PO Box 579, Gosford, NSW 2250, Australia

Scholastic New Zealand Limited
Private Bag 94407, Greenmount, Auckland, New Zealand

Scholastic Children's Books
Euston House, 24 Eversholt Street, London NW1 1DB, UK

Library and Archives Canada Cataloguing in Publication
Becker, Helaine, 1961-
The emperor strikes out / Helaine Becker ; illustrated by Sampar.
(Looney Bay All-Stars ; 5)
ISBN 978-0-545-99731-7
I. Sampar II. Title. III. Series: Becker, Helaine, 1961- . Looney Bay All-Stars ; 5
PS8553.E295532E46 2007   jC813'.6   C2007-902215-4
ISBN 10: 0-545-99731-3

6 5 4 3 2 1   Printed in Canada   07 08 09 10 11

Contents

Chapter 1 1

Chapter 2 10

Chapter 3 16

Chapter 4 27

Chapter 5 33

Chapter 6 46

Chapter 7 52

Chapter 8 60

Chapter 1

"Construction on the Roman Colosseum began in 72 A.D. The building was 48 metres high. The floor was sand. In fact, the word 'arena' actually means 'sand' . . ." Reese's teacher, Mr. Norman, droned from the front of the class.

Reese stared out the window. He tried to pay attention, he really did, but all he could think about was his mysterious, magical coin. The coin that seemed to bring people from other times to Looney Bay. The one that had somehow wound up in the soccer bag of Seamus "Snotty" Snodgrass, Reese's arch-enemy from Trinity Bay Prep School.

I have to get that coin back! Reese seethed. *Who knows what might happen if Seamus figures out what the coin can do?*

"Mr. McSkittles," scolded Mr. Norman, snapping Reese back to attention. "Can you tell us which emperor built the Roman Colosseum?"

"Um ... the Emperor Penguin?" Reese offered.

The class broke into peals of laughter.

"Very amusing," said Mr. Norman

sourly. "I hope you'll find detention just as funny."

Reese sighed. It was going to be another one of those days.

There had been a lot of "those days" ever since Reese had found the coin under a bench at the Looney Bay hockey arena.

First he'd been kidnapped by pirates and held captive aboard their ship. He had barely managed to survive that scrape. Then, medieval knights had shown up and Reese had found himself in the middle of their duel to the death! Next came the Vikings and the Skraelings, and after that, a famished fifteenth-century explorer named John Cabot. Reese's whole life had been turned upside down since he'd discovered the

coin. He wished he could get rid of it —
but not by handing it over to Seamus!

"What's bothering you?" Reese's
friend Darren asked later that day.
They were the last two kids to leave the
school. Darren had also gotten detention — during art class he had built a
model Colosseum out of clay and then
bombarded it with
pencil "spears." His
teacher had not
been impressed.
"You're not still
thinking about
that coin, are you?"

Reese nodded.

"I say good riddance," said Darren. He
followed Reese across the vacant lot
behind the schoolyard. "It's not your

problem anymore, so forget about it!"

"I wish I could!" Reese said. "But I feel responsible. I mean, it was my coin in the first place. And now if anything bad happens . . . "

"It won't be your fault," insisted Darren. "It will be —"

"His." Reese suddenly pointed and glared. Seamus was ahead of them, climbing the path up to Ebbert's Field.

Darren gulped. "Uh-oh," he said. He grabbed Reese's arm. "Don't do anything dumb!" he urged.

Reese shrugged him off. "Seamus! Wait up!" he called out.

A look of surprise crossed Seamus's face, but it was almost immediately replaced with a sneer. Seamus's bully-boy sidekicks, Jack Patrick and Roman Quaig,

appeared at his side. They folded their
arms and sneered too.

"What's the matter, Reesy, lost your
pieces?" mocked Seamus.

"Reese's Pieces!" Jack guffawed.
"That's a good one."

Reese ignored the jibe. "It's about
that coin you found in your soccer bag."

Seamus rolled his eyes. "Not *that*

again. You expect me to hand it over just because you say it's yours? No way! That coin looks really ancient. I bet it's worth a fortune. I'm going to get my dad to have it appraised."

"But Seamus," Reese said, "It *is* my coin. And it's special . . . "

"I'll say," said Seamus. "It's awesome. Look at how it sparkles." He dug the coin from his pocket and held it up to the sun. It glinted like a cat's eye. "I bet you wish you had a coin just like this," he taunted.

Seamus's words were just a roar in Reese's ears. Reese was captivated by the coin. He couldn't take his eyes off it.

He had to get it back!

Reese snatched the coin from Seamus's hand. He took off as fast as he could, running as if his life depended on it.

"Stop him!" yelled Seamus to his cronies. "He's got my coin!"

Chapter 2

Reese could hear the two boys thundering behind him. He felt rough hands grip his shirt. Then he was on the ground, his face in the dirt.

Seamus strolled over, not a hair out of place. He put his foot on the small of Reese's back.

"Give it back," Seamus said.

Reese struggled to get free.

"I said give it back," Seamus repeated,

pressing his foot harder into Reese's spine.

Darren rushed up. "Let him go!" He said, trying to yank Seamus away from Reese. "We're supposed to be civilized Canadians, not a bunch of bloodthirsty gladiators. Why don't you creepos start acting like it?"

"Who's gonna make us?" said Seamus. "There's three of us. And only two of you."

"Nice sportsmanlike conduct from the Captain of the Trinity Bay Marauders softball team," said Darren, shaking his head. "I'm sure your coach would like to hear about how you beat us up in an unfair fight."

Jack and Roman exchanged uneasy glances. A report like that could get the boys kicked off their team for good!

Seamus let Reese go. Reese rolled over, then got to his feet, thrust out his jaw and stood nose to nose with his enemy. He gripped the coin hard in his hand.

"I'll challenge you for the coin, Seamus, but not in a free-for-all like this," Reese said.

"So you think you're some sort of noble gladiator now?" jeered Seamus. "Fine then, I'll be *glad* to. I'll kick your can from here to Bonavista."

"Maybe," said Reese, "but if I win, the coin will be mine."

"Just name the time and place, glad-lad," said Seamus.

At that very moment, a bone-chilling roar filled the air. It sounded frighteningly close. Everyone froze.

"What the heck was that?" asked a panicky Darren.

"A moose?" suggested Jack.

"It sounded like a lion," whispered Darren.

"There are no lions in Newfoundland," said Reese. "Unless . . ."

"No. No no no no no!" cried Darren.

"The coin," breathed Reese.

Another blood-curdling roar pierced the air.

What had the coin conjured this time?

Reese ran up to the crest of the hill, where, larger than life, stood the *Roman Colosseum!*

Chapter 3

The Colosseum loomed over them, so huge it blotted out the sun.

"This can't be happening," Seamus said, rubbing his eyes.

"I told you the coin was special," Reese smirked.

"I think the roars are coming from inside it," said Darren. "Mr. Norman said they used to feed slaves and criminals to lions back then to entertain the Roman Emperor!"

"Ew! That's gross!" said Jack, wrinkling his nose.

"Thank goodness we don't have any slaves here in Newfoundland," said Reese.

"*Run, guys! Run!*" The boys turned and saw Laura Hook. She, along with two other teammates from the Looney Bay All-Stars, Randall Wetherbury and

Shannon Weiss, were being dragged uphill by a burly man in a leather jerkin!

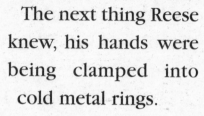

The next thing Reese knew, his hands were being clamped into cold metal rings.

"Good thing we rounded up these new ones so fast," barked one of the Roman slave traders. "They'll be ready just in time."

"What's going on? Just in time for what?" whined Seamus as chains snapped onto his wrists too. "I'm gonna call my dad!"

Laura said, "Yeah? Exactly how?" She held up her chained hands.

Then she turned to Reese. "These slimedogs nabbed us just after we left school. Then they saw you coming. We tried to warn you, but this slobberhead over here kept stuffing leaves in our mouths." Laura glared at her captor.

"Enough of this jabber," said Salivacus, the tallest slave trader. "We don't want to keep the Emperor waiting!" He grinned at his partner, Drulicus.

The Roman slavers prodded the kids toward the Colosseum. Another roar pierced the air. Then it was drowned out by a second roar — the roar of an excited crowd.

"Sounds like another slave just became kitty chow," chortled Salivacus.

"Oh goodie," replied Drulicus, licking his lips. "That's my favourite. Usually *lots* of gore."

The kids were dragged kicking and screaming into the bowels of the building. It was dark and dank. It smelled like a litter box. They could hear the moans of other captives.

Salivacus used an iron key to open a cell door. He shoved the kids in.

"Enjoy your last hour, folks. We've got Barbarian gladiators from the just-annexed Province of Lanso up next. They're a fierce lot. If you're not fed to the lions first, I expect those brutes will be turning you all into mincemeat soon enough," he grunted.

"Who else is here?" called out Laura.

"Nobody but us slaves, Ma'am," came a voice from the next cell. "But you really needn't bother with us. We're up next. You see, since Emperor Zero is here today, they're pulling out all the stops. We should be done like dinner by sundown. You might as well say your prayers too."

Salivacus and Drulicus laughed uproariously.

"Pray away! Don't mind us," said Salivacus. He leaned against the damp stone wall. He casually tossed a coin in the air as he chuckled to himself.

Reese peered through the gloom at Salivacus. The way the coin glinted in the streaky light sneaking from the narrow window above him was strangely familiar. If Reese didn't know it was safely tucked in his own pocket, he would have sworn it was his own coin!

Seamus noticed Salivacus's coin too. With chains clanking, he edged closer.

"What have you got there?" he asked.

"You mean this?" Salivacus asked, holding up the coin.

Seamus nodded and swallowed hard.

"It's only an *uncia*. I got bags of 'em."

He patted a leather satchel hanging from his belt. "My pay for rounding up you feline feed."

"Lemme see that," said Seamus. He snatched the coin from Salivacus's hand. "This looks exactly like the coin I found!"

Salivacus snarled at Seamus. He reached for the coin. Before he could grab it back, the cell echoed with a strange hum.

Reese stared at the coin in Seamus's fingers. As he looked, the coin seemed to emit a shimmering light. Suddenly, the coin in Reese's pocket began to jiggle. His pocket shook like it was possessed. Reese tried to hold it still with his chained hands, but the coin seemed to have gained a life of its own.

It wriggled itself out of the pocket and into Reese's hand. Everyone stopped and stared.

A fierce wind swirled in the cell. The coin in Seamus's hand went *zing*! through the air and WHOMP! right into Reese's hand beside his own coin.

The two coins glowed and danced in Reese's palm. Then they began to morph. Where there had been two

coins, now there was only one large one. They had fused together!

"Why you little thief!" growled Salivacus, sticking his arms through the bars and gripping Seamus by the throat. "As punishment, we'll put you in against the Barbarians next!"

Chapter 4

"B-b-but I didn't mean to do it!" Seamus blubbered. "Honest! I just wanted to s-s-see your coin, I swear!"

"You can swear all you want, by Jupiter! It won't do you any good. The Emperor wants to see a good old Barbarian blood 'n' guts rampage today. So that's enough of your magic tricks. Say goodbye to your chums. Though you'll be seeing each other on the other

side of the River Styx soon enough, *heh heh*."

"Where's that?" Darren whispered to Laura.

"I think he means in the under-world," she replied.

"I was afraid of that," Darren moaned.

Reese felt terrible. It was *his* fault Seamus was about to be sliced like salami by Barbarian butchers. It was true that Snotty Snodgrass was not his favourite person in the world. But even so, he didn't deserve to become Barbarian barbecue.

Do something, do something, Reese thought to himself. *But what?*

"Is death and dismemberment the only kind of entertainment you lame-os can come up with?" Reese blurted. "Brutality is *sooo* yesterday. Practically ancient history."

Randall tried to clamp his hand over Reese's mouth, but the chains got in the way. Reese went on. "I bet the Emperor would prefer to see something different."

"Oh yeah?" said Salivacus. "What makes you so smart?"

"I'm from Canada," Reese said, "where people know how to have a really good time. A little fiddle music, a little dancing ... a little ... baseball! Now that's some fun, isn't it, gang?"

"You bet!" said Darren, giving Reese the thumbs up.

"Absolutely," agreed Randall.

"Don't you think so too, Seamus?" Laura asked, kicking him in the shin.

Seamus, who was still staring goggle-eyed at the coin in Reese's hand, stammered, "Um . . . well, yeah! Everybody loves baseball!"

Salivacus stroked his hoary chin. "I wonder," he said, "if maybe the Emperor wouldn't pay an extra *uncia* or two for a novelty . . . "

Reese saw his chance. "Baseball, baseball, baseball!" he chanted.

The Looney Bay All-Stars joined in. "Baseball, baseball, baseball!"

Then the slaves added to the chorus: "Baseball, baseball, baseball!"

Salivacus nodded. "Okay. We'll try it. If Emperor Zero gives you the thumbs up, you'll all go free."

"What if Zero gives us the thumbs down?" Darren asked nervously.

"Why, then we give all of you to the Barbarians!" Salivacus exclaimed. "You have five *minutae* to prepare. May the gods be with you!"

Chapter 5

"Gather round!" Reese called to the slaves. "Lemme run through the rules: The pitcher throws the ball . . ."

"What's a pitcher?" asked a slave called Yehuda.

"The pitcher is the person who throws the ball."

"So why don't you call him the thrower, then?"

"Because in baseball, you don't throw the ball, you 'pitch' the ball," replied Reese.

"I don't understand," interrupted Yehuda. "First you said, 'the pitcher throws the ball.' Now you're saying you *don't* throw the ball."

"You *do* throw the ball. In baseball, we call a throw a pitch. The thrower is called the pitcher."

"Ahhh!" said Yehuda. "So what do you call the person who catches the ball, then?"

"The catcher," Reese said. "Now can you let me finish? We only have five minutes before Saliva boy comes back to get us, and you don't even know —"

"Fine." Yehuda sniffed. "You don't have to get all testy with us. It's not like

you're any better than us, you know.
You're future Barbarian barbecue too."

 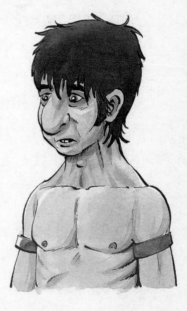

"None of us will be!" insisted Laura.
"Not if we do this right! So listen up!"

"Okay, so the pitcher pitches the ball.
The ball has to go right over the plate.
The batter gets three chances to hit the
ball —"

But before Reese could finish, Salivacus and Drulicus returned. The captives were shoved out into the arena. Thousands upon thousands of Romans hooted and hollered at them.

Drulicus unchained their hands. Salivacus poked at Reese, ordering him to explain the game of baseball to the crowd.

Meanwhile, Randall ran out to the field. He used the heel of his shoe to draw the baselines. Darren folded up some togas to make bases. Laura filled a sheep's bladder with water to use as the ball. Shannon borrowed some padded leather satchels from Drulicus. She handed them out to use as mitts. One of Drulicus's clubs served as the bat.

Then Drulicus divided the captives into two even teams.

Seamus and Jack were put on the same team as Reese and Laura.

Seamus gave Reese an evil glare.

"Yeah, I don't like having to team up with you either," Reese said. "But we're just going to have to suck it up and work together. Do you think you Marauders can handle that?"

Reluctantly, Seamus nodded.

"Yeah, I don't want to battle Barbarians," Jack agreed.

"Then let's play our best! Go All-Stars! Go Marauders! Go team!" Reese chanted. Laura put her hand out. Seamus reached across and laid his hand on top of hers. Then the rest of the team gathered around. They put their hands out, one on top of the other.

"Go team! Go team! Go team!" they all chanted.

The crowd booed. Where was the novelty in this? Where was the excitement?

"Bring on the Barbarians!" someone shouted from the stands.

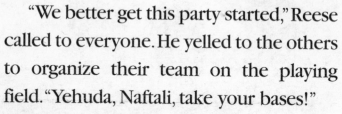

A squishy, rotten fig hit Reese right in the ear.

"We better get this party started," Reese called to everyone. He yelled to the others to organize their team on the playing field. "Yehuda, Naftali, take your bases!"

The next thing Reese knew, Yehuda was bringing him the toga Darren had folded for first base.

"What are you doing, Yehuda?" Reese bellowed in exasperation.

"You said take your bases!" Yehuda replied. "So I did. And please — call me Hu. Everyone does."

"I didn't mean *pick up* the bases. I meant you should take your places on the infield! You'll have to put the bases back. So," Reese continued, "Who's on first?"

"Okay," said Hu.

"Okay what?" Reese asked, puzzled.

"You said Hu's on first. So I agreed with you," said Hu.

"Aaargh!" Reese pulled his hair in frustration. The crowd booed even louder. The Emperor seemed bored. He was holding a lute in his hand and was starting to rub his sceptre distractedly along its strings.

"That doesn't look good," said Darren, pointing out the Emperor's yawns to Reese. "Any minute now he's going to give us the thumbs down."

"We better get started! Hu, just go to the pitcher's mound and throw the ball. Can you do that?"

"Sure, but who will be on first?"

"Whoever you want," Reese said, shaking his head as he jogged to the dugout.

Seamus batted first. Hu threw an easy blooper right at him. Seamus struck the ball squarely. It exploded, splashing water and sheep goo all over him.

The Emperor laughed. The crowd laughed too.

"Good work!" shouted Shannon from first base. "Try using this instead, though!" She tossed him a knotted ball of rope she had found lying near her

feet — one of the lions' toys.

Hu pitched again. This time, when Seamus hit it, the ball sailed deep into the stands!

The crowd let out a roar of appreciation. The Emperor nodded and smiled as Seamus trotted around the bases.

Next up was Reese. Hu's pitch blazed by Reese, catching him looking. Strike one!

The second pitch was a curveball, low and away. Reese swung and missed! Strike two!

"Come on, Reese, you can do it!" shouted Shannon.

Hu wound up and threw again. The ball seemed to hang just over the plate. Reese closed his eyes and swung with all his might. *Bammo*! The ball was going . . . going . . . THWACK!

The ball smacked Emperor Zero right between the eyes!

Chapter
6

A terrible silence washed over the
Colosseum. Zero teetered from his seat,
bounced twice, and rolled to a stop
next to the pine nut vendor. His pre-
cious lute slipped from his grasp. It
bounced twice too. It landed at Reese's
feet. The sceptre fell with a *twang* on
the lute's strings. For a moment, nothing
happened. Then the Emperor groaned.
He rubbed his forehead and rose to his

feet. He glowered at Reese.

Everyone in the Colosseum held their breath. Emperor Zero slowly raised his hand. He was just about to give the thumbs down sign, when Reese got a "twang" of inspiration.

He picked up the lute. He brought it to his chin. Using the sceptre as a bow, he started to fiddle. It sounded awful at first, like the yowling of a sick cat. But after a few moments, Reese managed to eke out some familiar notes. Pretty soon the Looney Bay kids realized Reese was playing Newfoundland's own beloved tune, "I's the B'y."

"Come on, everybody, we gotta help Reese!" Darren encouraged. As Reese fiddled for his life, Darren launched into

a traditional jig. Then Shannon's sweet soprano voice rang out clear and strong:

"I's the b'y that builds the boat
And I's the b'y that sails her
I's the b'y that catches the fish
And brings them home to Lizer."

The rest of the kids, including the Marauders, joined in for the chorus.

"Hip yer partner, Sally Tibbo
Hip yer partner, Sally Brown
Fogo, Twillingate, Moreton's Harbour
All around the circle!"

Zero's shoulders started to bobble up and down. The mad Emperor was giggling!

He stuck out his thumb. The thumb went . . .

UP! The kids were saved!

"Woohoo!" they shouted. Reese bowed to Zero and handed the fiddle-lute back to him. Zero gave him a tiny nod of acknowledgement.

"The rest of you slaves! Your time is up! Send in the Barbarians, Drulicus!" barked Salivacus.

Yehuda fell to his knees at Reese's feet. He clutched at Reese's shirt.

"Don't let them kill us!" pleaded Yehuda. "Help us! Please!"

"Think of something, Reese!" begged Shannon. "We can't just let them get

dismembered out there!"

"But what can we do?" cried Reese. "I'm all out of ideas!"

A somber drum roll sounded.

Boom ... boom ... boom ...

Reese heard the ominous creak of gates opening.

Boom ... boom ... boom ...

The Barbarians were at the gate!

Chapter 7

Reese stared in shock. The Barbarians were none other than Leif Ericsson and the rest of Reese's Viking pals!

"Hot herring in lingonberry sauce!" Reese whistled. "Look who's here! When Salivacus said, 'the Province of Lanso,' he must have meant L'anse aux Meadows! Hey! Leif! Thorvald! Long time no see!" Reese hailed his friends.

Leif's face lit up.

"Reese? Is that you? And Laura . . . ? And Darren . . . ? And aren't those the cheaters from the Marauders?"

"Yeah, but listen, we've got a bit of a situation here," Reese said, drawing Leif aside.

"*Ja, ja,*" Leif said, nodding and stroking his beard as Reese explained what had happened.

"No, of course we can not kill these

poor slaves," Leif agreed. "We did not know this was not a Canadian event. And that these people were calling us 'Barbarians.' This is not very nice."

"Slaughter them! Slaughter them!" the crowd started chanting.

Leif cast a cool eye over the crowd. "They call *us* the Barbarians. Listen to these people! We Vikings never behave like such animals. And smell the air in here. *Feh*! Don't these piggy-wiggies ever take a bath?"

Leif strode over to Emperor Zero. Before any of the imperial guards could react, he was holding Zero by back of his toga.

"This is not a country for the blood-shed, *ja*?" said Leif. "This is a civilized land, like Rome is *supposed* to be. No looting! No pillaging! No slaughter either! And why are you here anyway, you crazy man?" Leif continued. "Don't you know Rome is burning! That's what I heard on the CBC, anyway. You go home and save your city, *ja*?"

Zero's eyes brightened. He looked crazier than ever. "I love fire!" he exulted.

"Um, excuse me, Mr. Barbarian," Yehuda said, tugging on Leif's tunic. "But we don't want to go back to Rome. You know what they do to slaves like us back there. And our new buddies, these taskmasters, they don't want to go either."

"That's true," agreed Salivacus. "I never wanted to be a slave trader. I always wanted to be an actor. But slave trading was the family business. We couldn't refuse dear old Dad."

"I've got it!" exclaimed Reese. "Leif, why don't you take them back to Norstead with you?"

"Norstead? What's that?" asked Salivacus.

"It's a wonderful village up the coast," Reese began.

"*Ja*, with lots of shiny clean girls, and lots of work for strong men and actors. Who wants to go?"

"I certainly do," Hu said.

"Me too," said Naftali.

"And us!" the rest of the slaves chimed.

"Great idea," said Seamus, "but how do we get rid of the Colosseum?"

"Good question," said Reese. "We really don't know how this thing works," he said, fingering the coin.

"We sent the explorer John Cabot back in time, though, when we chucked the coin into the ocean," Randall ventured. "Maybe we can try pitching the coin away again."

"Good idea. It's worth a try anyway." said Reese. He fished the coin out of his pocket and held it up. "Here goes nothing," he muttered under his breath.

With all his might, Reese hurled the coin high into the air. Up, up, it went, spinning like a twinkly golden planet.

It landed in the dirt at Reese's feet with a soft *whoompf*. Nothing happened.

Zero cleared his throat and rose to his feet. "Let us depart!" he intoned, raising his jewelled hand in the air.

Then, suddenly, the air seemed to shimmer. The coin seemed to rise up into the air. A loud *whoosh* filled the stadium.

A moment later, Reese and his friends were standing in an empty field, the wind howling around them.

Chapter 8

"Whoa, that was weird," Reese said into the silence. He picked up the coin and stuffed it into his pocket. Was it the coin that spirited the Colosseum away, or Zero's words? Reese had no clue. The more experiences he had with the coin, the less he seemed to understand its mysterious ways.

Leif took instant command of the

Roman slaves and slavers.

"Finish off the hand holding, *ja*? It is done. We must go! Ingmar waits with the ship in the Looney Bay."

Zero's lute and sceptre were lying on the ground. Yehuda picked them up.

"Looks like Zero forgot something," he said. "You know, I liked that little ditty you played, Reese. There's another

tune that keeps going through my head, though. I wouldn't mind trying it out."

Yehuda lifted the lute to his chin the way Reese had. He stroked the sceptre across the strings. He hummed a few notes, and then started to play. It sounded a lot like "O Canada."

"That's going to be real popular around here," said Reese, clapping him on the back. "Why don't you take that fiddle with you, Hu."

"Thanks," said Hu.

"Any time you come to Norstead, be sure to visit us!" Leif said to the All-Stars. "Even *you* will be welcome," he said and nodded to the Marauders. "Now let's go! Left! Right! Left! Right!"

"Goodbye! Goodbye!" everyone shouted as the Vikings and the Romans

disappeared in the twilight.

"I guess it's time for us to head home too," said Randall.

Seamus shuffled his feet. "Um, can I talk to you a second, Reese?"

"Sure," Reese replied.

"That was some quick thinking you

did back there. Maybe you're, er, not such a, you know, twit, after all."

Reese felt his cheeks get hot. "Aw, it was nothing," he said, surprised. "But thanks anyway."

For a second, it looked like the two boys might shake hands, or worse, hug. But then Darren exploded in a fit of fake coughing. Reese and Seamus turned away from each other in embarrassment.

It was almost dark, and the air was still and cool. Darren and Reese walked side by side through the gathering shadows.

"What are you going to do with the coin, Reese?" Darren asked.

"I dunno. Stuff it in a drawer and never touch it again," Reese replied.

An eerie roar echoed over the hills. They froze.

"Did you hear what I heard?" asked Darren.

"It sure sounded like a lion," said Reese. "Do you think one might have got left behind by mistake?"

Darren chuckled nervously. "I hope not. But if one did, there will be some mighty surprised moose tonight, eh?"